The Most Beautiful Place in the World

The Most Beautiful Place in the World

Ann Cameron

Drawings by Thomas B. Allen

YOUNG CORGI

THE MOST BEAUTIFUL PLACE IN THE WORLD

A YOUNG CORGI BOOK 0 552 52601 0

First published in USA by Alfred A. Knopf, Inc., 1988
First published in UK by Doubleday, a division of Transworld Publishers Ltd.,
by arrangement with Alfred A. Knopf, Inc.

PRINTING HISTORY
Doubleday edition published 1989
Young Corgi edition published 1992
Reprinted 1993

Text copyright © 1988 by Ann Cameron
Illustrations copyright © 1988 by Thomas B. Allen
Cover illustration by Kim Harley

Young Corgi Books are published by Transworld Publishers Ltd., 61–63
Uxbridge Road, Ealing, London W5 5SA, in Australia by Transworld
Publishers (Australia) Pty. Ltd., 15–25 Helles Avenue, Moorebank, NSW 2170,
and in New Zealand by Transworld Publishers (N.Z.) Ltd., 3 William
Pickering Drive, Albany, Auckland

Printed and bound in Great Britain by
Cox & Wyman Ltd., Reading, Berks.

FOR PABLO ZAVALA,

who introduced me to Guatemala

– A.C.

The Most Beautiful Place in the World

My name is Juan. I live in Guatemala, in the mountains. My town, San Pablo, has three huge volcanoes near it, and high cliffs all around it, and steep, bright green fields of corn and garlic and onions growing in the hills, and red coffee berries growing in the shade of big trees in the valleys. It has lots of flowers and birds — eagles and orioles and owls, hummingbirds, and flocks of wild parrots that zoom down out of the trees to steal our corn and don't talk any language but their own.

San Pablo is on a big lake with seven other towns around it. People get from one town to another mostly by ferry-boat or canoe. There's a road, but it's not a good one.

I've never been in any of the other towns, only San Pablo. Still, at night I like to go down to the lake and look at the lights of the fishing canoes on the black water, and the lights of the other towns glowing at us across the lake, and the thousands of stars in the sky. It seems like every light is saying, 'You're not alone. We're here too.'

Right in town, San Pablo has stray dogs and dust in the street, and a few cars, and a few buses from the big cities, and a few mules carrying firewood from the mountains, and lots of people carrying still more stuff – jugs of water or big baskets of bread or vegetables on their heads, babies on their backs, or sometimes huge wooden beams balanced over their shoulders – whatever they need to take home. Since there aren't many cars, if you want something, you carry it yourself, no matter how heavy it is.

The only time people aren't carrying things is at night, when they go out just to stroll around town and have fun and tell stories and talk to their friends. Everybody walks in the street, more or

14

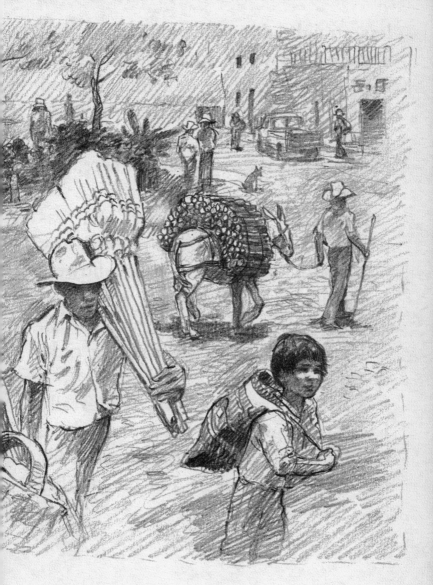

15

less straight down the middle, and if a car comes while somebody's having a good conversation or telling a good story, the car has to wait till the story finishes before people will move out of the way. Stories are important here, and cars aren't.

Down by the beach there's an especially beautiful place – a big, low house with lots of windows, and flowers and palm trees all around, and green grass and peacocks in the yard, and an iron gate that opens for walking right down to the water.

That's where I was born. Well, really I was born in a little house behind the big house. My dad was the caretaker for the big house, and he and my mother had the little house at the back to live in, for free. But after I was born, my dad wanted to go out with his friends at night the way he did when he was single, and my mother said there wasn't enough money for that, so they fought, and one day my dad just left. I heard he took the bus to the capital, which is not that far away; but he never came back to see my mum or me. The truth is, I remember the peacocks on the lawn where we lived better than I remember my dad.

After my dad left, the rich people who owned the big house had to hire a new caretaker, and naturally they wanted him to live in our little house, so my mother had to move out. She was only seventeen, and she didn't have any money or any way to take care of me, so she took me and moved back home to my grandmother's house. My grandfather died a long time ago, but lucky for us, my grandmother isn't poor. She has a house made out of cement blocks, with windows without any glass in them – they have little wooden shutters that my grandmother closes at night or when it rains. The house has four rooms, and all the walls inside are covered with the paintings my Uncle Miguel has made, which are really pretty, and which he says he's going to sell one day.

Outside, my grandmother keeps lots of flowers, so the house looks nice. But best of all, my grandmother owns her house and the land it's on. She keeps the papers that prove it in an iron box under her bed, and she's sure of what they say because somebody she trusts read them to her, and nobody, praise God, can take my grandmother's house and land away from her.

My grandmother's house is big, but it's pretty crowded, because my three unmarried uncles, and sometimes some of my five married aunts and their kids, live with us too. Sometimes even my grandmother's cousins' kids have lived with us for a while. In fact, if anybody in the family loses a job, or gets sick, or can't get along with a husband, or has some kind of trouble, they come to live with my grandmother. She takes care of everybody, until they can take care of

20

themselves again. Sometimes, though, you can tell she wishes they would get round to taking care of themselves sooner than they do.

My grandmother earns her living selling *arroz con leche* – rice with milk – in the big market where everyone goes to buy food every day. *Arroz con leche* is like rice pudding, except you don't eat it with a spoon, you drink it hot in a glass. It's sweet, and it has lots of cinnamon in it, and my grandmother makes it better than anybody in town. She gets up at five in the morning every day to start making it. That's what she's done, almost every day of her life, since she was thirteen years old.

After my mum and I moved back to

my grandmother's, I'd wake up in the morning in bed with my mother and hear the sounds of everybody getting up – Uncle Miguel muttering, 'Where's my shoe, my shoe, my shoe?' and my Aunt Maria whispering to her son Carlitos, 'You *didn't* wet the bed again, did you?' and Angelica, my Aunt Tina's fat little daughter, crying because she doesn't want to take a shower; and I'd smell the wood of the cooking fire, and the *arroz con leche* steaming in a big, smoke-blackened pot, and the breakfast tortillas toasting; and then my mother and I would take our towel and get our turn in the shower. My grandmother has running water in her house, which most people don't. She says she needs it for the *arroz con leche* business. But she doesn't have electricity, or hot water in the shower. She says electricity and hot water and things like that are expensive, and not very important.

So my mum and I lived in my grandmother's house, and my mum earned some money cleaning houses and washing people's clothes in the big wash-tub at the back of the house; and at night she'd take me out to walk around town, and we'd meet all her friends and talk to them, and it was fun.

One night when we were out like that, a man came up to my mother with a big smile on his face. He said, 'What a good-looking boy you have! He certainly resembles you!' And then he bought me some sweets, and talked to my mother some more.

Pretty soon every night that we went out, we'd see him, and he'd walk with us. Then one night he invited my mum to a dance. After the night of the dance, she started leaving me at home when she went out. I suppose she wanted to see him alone.

All of a sudden one day, she told me she was going to get married again to that man we met on the street. She was going to go and live with him. But I couldn't go with her. He didn't want me. He wanted to start his own family. He wanted his own children. He didn't have the money for me.

And that same day, my mother moved

out of my grandmother's house and moved in with my stepfather. He had a house, but just one room. And he didn't have a bed, so he and my mum came up to my grandmother's house, and he and my mother carried out the bed she and I had been sleeping in and took it down to his house. My grandmother wasn't home when they came for the bed, or maybe she wouldn't have let them take it.

When they were carrying the bed, I followed them out to the road, but my mother said, 'You stay here, Juan,' so I went back to the house.

Once they were gone, I didn't know what to do, so I just hung around all day until my grandmother came home, and went up to her and pulled her into the room where our bed used to be.

My grandmother frowned. 'So now you have no bed!' she said. I started to cry. It's bad enough not having a father and a mother, but when you don't even have a place to sleep, it's worse.

When I stopped crying, I asked my grandmother if I could sleep with her at night, but she said no.

'I have to work too hard,' she said. 'I need my rest. I have had enough sleeping with children. Children kick,' she said.

'I won't kick,' I said.

'You say you won't, but in your sleep you would,' my grandmother said.

She could see I was going to cry again.

'But just a minute,' she said. 'We'll fix up something for you.'

And she looked around and found a bunch of empty rice bags, and put them on the floor by her bed, and gave me a blanket off her bed. She got everything all ready for me before dinner, about five in the afternoon. I guess she knew I was worried that I didn't have a place where I belonged any more, and if I at least had a place to sleep, I wouldn't be so scared.

Then she told me, 'Well, Grandson, you can stay here, but you know the rule about the gate. You have to obey the rule about the gate, you know.'

I nodded and said, 'Yes, Grandma.'

My grandmother's house has a high

fence around it, and a wooden gate with a lock on it that my grandmother locks every night. The only ones besides her who have keys are my uncles. Everyone else has to be in by eight thirty. After that, my grandmother won't get up to let them in. No matter how hard anyone knocks, she just shuts her ears. And she won't let anyone else go and open the gate either.

I told my grandmother I understood about the gate, but since I was still little, maybe I didn't exactly understand.

Once my mother was gone, I started going for walks alone after dinner. I didn't really belong to anyone, so I did whatever I wanted.

One night a few days after my mother

left, I went for a really long walk, all the way to the lake. By the time I got back to my grandmother's house, it had been dark a long time, and the gate was locked.

I didn't know what to do. And I was cold, besides. I just had shorts and a T–shirt on, and even though San Pablo is hot during the day, it gets cold at night because we're so high up in the mountains.

The only thing I could think of to do was to look for my mother. I knew where my stepfather's house was, so I decided to go there. When I got there, through the window I saw a candle burning. Nobody ever goes to sleep or goes outside leaving a candle burning, because it could burn up everything in the house. So I knew somebody was awake, and inside.

I wasn't tall enough to see who, so I put a rock below the window and stood on it to look in. I saw my mother, alone.

I knocked once, so softly she didn't hear me, and then once again, louder.

My mother opened the door a crack, and saw me. All she said was 'You!'

Of course, my mother knew the rule about the gate, and how late it was, and how I must have got locked out.

She stood for a minute in the doorway, and then she said, 'Come on in.' She could see I was shivering. Sometimes when you shiver, it's not just from the cold.

Inside the house there was a table with the candle, two stools, two plates, two cups, and some bananas. There were a few clothes hanging on nails in the wall, and a little rug on the floor, and, of

course, the bed. That was all. The room could have used a lot of other stuff. Mainly, the one thing I wished it had was a back door for me to go out through if my stepfather came in through the front door.

'You can stay here,' my mother said, 'but if your stepfather sees you when he comes home, he'll get very angry and hit you. So you'll have to hide, and sleep under the bed.'

So I got down on the floor under the bed, back against the wall out of sight, and my mother shook out the little rug to make it cleaner and put it over me.

But I couldn't go to sleep, because I was afraid of what would happen when my stepfather came home.

After quite a while there was a loud knock on the door, and my mother unbolted it. From where I was, I could just see my stepfather's legs and feet coming into the house. Then I heard him kiss my mum.

'The man finally showed up and paid me the money he owed me,' my stepfather said. 'So tomorrow you can buy the things you need.'

'Good!' my mother said, and then they talked a little about what they'd buy for the house.

'The candle's going out,' my stepfather said. 'Time to turn in for the night.'

I watched his feet coming closer and closer. The bed creaked as he sat down on it. He took his shoes off and put his bare feet on the floor.

'Where's the rug?' he asked.

'I washed it,' my mother said. 'It's outside. It's still wet.'

'Well, we don't need it,' my step-father said, and they both went to bed, and I went to sleep.

In the morning my mother woke me early, before my stepfather woke up. I crawled out from under the bed without saying a word, trying to be perfectly quiet. My mother unbolted the door and I tiptoed out.

'Remember,' my mother whispered, 'you can't come here again!'

She closed the door, and I ran up the road all the way to my grandmother's house.

'Where were you?' my grandmother said.

'At my mother's house.'

'And what happened?' my grandmother asked.

'Nothing,' I said. 'Only I can't go there again.'

I thought I never would. But the next night my grandmother took me by the hand and said, 'Come with me,' and we walked to my mother's house.

My grandmother knocked on the door, slowly, three times.

My mother opened the door. My stepfather was behind her, sitting on the bed, but he stood up when he saw my grandmother.

'How are you, Mother?' my mother said. She and my stepfather looked nervous, but my grandmother didn't.

'I'm fine, as always,' my grandmother said, 'but your son needs a bed, and you must get him one.' She turned around and put her hand on my shoulder and we left.

Sure enough, they did get me a bed, and they brought it up to my grandmother's house the next week. It was a wooden bed, and all the legs were slightly different lengths, but my Uncle Luis borrowed a saw and fixed it up for me.

After that, I only saw my mother by

accident, in the street. She always said, 'How are you, Juan?' as if she cared, but I only said, 'Fine, Mother,' and nothing else. One day when I saw her, I realized she was going to have a baby, and a few months later she had it. So I had a half brother, but he didn't know who I was. When I saw him at the side of the street playing, I wanted to knock him down and punch him – for having a mother, when I didn't. But I never hit him. He was just a little kid. I could see that nothing was his fault.

Anyway, my life wasn't so bad. I played football in the street with my cousins and the kids in the neighbourhood. My Uncle Rodolfo taught me how to do somersaults and backflips, and my

Uncle Miguel let me use his paints some-times. And a few times I went for walks with my aunts at night, the way I used to walk with my mother.

The other thing I did was help my grandmother in the market with the *arroz con leche*. I learned how to ladle it out, and how to give change and see that nobody took any when Grandma wasn't looking. And when I'd done that for a while, my grandmother told me she thought I was ready to have a job alone, and she taught me how to shine shoes, and bought me a shoeshine kit and a stool for customers to sit on, and the two of us worked out where I should stand to get the most business – by the Tourist Office and the giant photo of San Pablo

that has writing underneath it.

At the beginning my grandmother watched. The first two customers I did a good job for, and then, on the third pair of shoes, I skipped a little.

The customer said, 'Oh, that's OK.'
He was going to pay me anyway.

But my grandmother said, 'No, it's
not OK. He has to do them right, all
the time. He has to work well, all the

time. If he can't do that, he'll never earn a living.'

'OK,' said the customer. So I got his shoes perfect.

'Can you do that every time?' my grandmother asked, and I said yes, and she went back to her rice.

So I shined a lot of shoes, and pretty soon I earned about a dollar every day. Grown men only earn two dollars, so I was doing very well.

And I talked to people when I shined their shoes, and asked them where they lived, and what they did, and if they had kids. Working was fun. And I gave all the money to my grandmother. She always gave me a hug and a big smile, and let me keep ten cents for myself.

The only thing was, it got bad when I saw kids who were going past me on the way to school. I was sitting in the dust all smeared up with shoe polish, and they were all neat and clean, with their pencils and their notebooks, going to school.

A lot of kids don't go to school because their parents want them to work. The law is, they are supposed to go to school until they are twelve. But the school really doesn't have space for everyone, so nobody makes them go.

Most kids who work, work out in the country, in the onion fields, so I felt lonely when I watched the schoolkids going by.

And after a while I started wondering why my grandmother didn't send me to school. I started thinking, if she really loved me, she'd send me to school and not just have me shine shoes.

I wanted to ask her to let me go, but I was scared to. I was scared she'd say no. Then I would find out she liked me only because I was earning money for her. I'd find out she was like my father and mother and stepfather, who never cared about me. I'd find out she was just acting as if she loved me.

Then I told myself that my grandmother was good; she couldn't help it if she needed money more than I needed school. I decided school didn't matter. I decided I could learn to read by myself.

I asked my shoeshine customers what the letters were on the signs and pretty soon I could read every sign around: COCA-COLA, BANK OF GUATEMALA, TOURIST OFFICE, and even the writing under the picture of San Pablo.

When I ran out of signs, somebody gave me a newspaper, and I worked on reading that, and the customers helped me. I tore the newspaper into pages and always carried a page in my back pocket to work on. And soon I could read almost the whole thing. But when I wasn't reading, I was just sitting around, waiting for customers, wondering what kids did at school and whether my grandmother really loved me, and it seemed as though life had stopped,

because that was all I thought about.

Finally, I decided that I had to do it – go and ask my grandmother about school. I got a friend of mine, Roberto, an orphan who lives in the street, to guard my shoeshine stuff, and I went up to the market to talk to my grandmother.

She was surprised to see me, since I was supposed to be working.

'What's going on, Juan?' she said.

I said, 'Grandma, I want to go to school.'

'School?' She said it like I'd said I wanted to go to Mars. 'You can't go.'

'Yes, I can!' I said. 'All you have to do is take me!' I had thought I was ready for her to say no, but I wasn't.

'But you're too young,' she said. 'You're five.'

'Grandma,' I said, 'I'm not five, I'm seven!'

And it turned out that there were so many of us around, she had lost track of how old I was.

'Seven! Why didn't you tell me? There are too many of you. There's too much to remember. You should have told me!

'How long have you been seven?' she said, as if I had played some trick on her behind her back.

'Six months,' I said.

'And you waited all this time to tell me!'

'It was so important, I couldn't,' I said.

'When something's important, that's when you've got to say it!' my grandmother said. 'You've got to stand up for yourself. It doesn't even matter if you lose. What matters is that you never stop trying to get what you really want. Of course,' she added, 'I mean important things, not things like hot water and electricity.

'Well, if you really are seven, you must go to school,' my grandmother said. 'You should have been there long before this.'

The next morning I put on my clean clothes, not my shoeshining clothes, and before school started, my grandmother and I went to see the teacher, Doña Irene.

'I want to enter school,' I said.

'How old are you?' Doña Irene said.

'Seven and a half.'

'You're more than old enough,' Doña Irene said, 'but you can't begin now. Next year.'

She smiled goodbye and started looking through some papers on her desk.

My grandmother didn't move.

'He wants to go to school very, very much,' she said.

Doña Irene looked up politely, as if my grandmother had missed the point and should have left already.

'He's three months late for starting. The other children are doing arithmetic.'

'He knows arithmetic,' my grandmother said. 'He's worked with me in the market.'

'The others can read a little,' Doña Irene said. 'He'll never catch up.'

'He is ready for school,' my grandmother said. 'He will catch up.'

Doña Irene looked my grandmother in the eye, as if to say she knew who ran the school and it wasn't my grandmother.

'No,' she said.

'But I *can* read!' I said. And I pulled out the piece of newspaper from my back pocket and started reading it out loud.

Doña Irene looked very surprised. 'Well,' she said, 'in that case . . .'

So I was admitted into the first year.

I went to school from eight in the morning till two in the afternoon, and later I shined shoes. I had the money to buy books and notebooks and everything because my grandmother had saved what I had earned shoeshining, in her iron box.

When I'd been at school for two months, Doña Irene sent me home with a note to my grandmother. I showed it to her after supper, and she got my Aunt Tina to read it to her, even though I told her I could read it myself.

'No, Juan,' my grandmother said. 'It's about you, so you're not the one to read it.'

The note said that, with my grandmother's permission, the teachers wanted to move me into the second year. Doña Irene said that they had never had a pupil who had learned to read like I had, by myself, before ever starting school. She said that it would be a tragedy if such a good pupil had to leave school, and that if my grandmother ever could not keep me in school, the teachers would help to keep me there.

When Aunt Tina stopped reading, she looked at me as if she had never really seen me before, and was looking to see what was so special about me, and still couldn't see it, and gave up.

'Well, congratulations!' she said.

And I thought my grandmother would congratulate me too. But she

didn't, she started to cry, and threw her arms around me.

She said, 'When I was seven, the teachers went from house to house, looking for children to enrol in school, but when they got to my house, my parents hid me in the woodshed. I watched between cracks in the boards, and listened. They told the teachers that they didn't have any school–age children, not one. They did it because they were afraid if I went to school, I wouldn't learn to work. They did it for my good, and I didn't say anything or complain, but I always knew it was a mistake.'

She dried her eyes, and she told me she would help me study even all the way to university in the capital. As long as she lived she would help me, she said, if I did my best.

And she looked at me as if I were a man already, and said that maybe by studying I could find out why some people were rich, and some were poor, and some countries were rich, and some were poor, because she had thought about it a lot, but she could never understand it.

And I felt very proud, but also scared, because just more or less by accident I had taught myself to read, but that didn't mean I was so clever.

I said to my grandmother, 'I might not always do everything special.'

'You don't have to do everything special,' my grandmother said. 'Just your best. That's all.'

I was proud, but I wasn't so sure I wanted to do my best all the time. I thought it could get pretty inconvenient. If people started expecting a lot of me, I would have to do more and more.

'You ask more from me than Doña Irene and all the teachers,' I said. 'They don't expect so much.'

My grandmother glared at me. 'They don't love you the way I do either,' she said.

Then she said, 'Come on, let's go for a walk.'

She put on her best shawl, and she and I went down the street together, and she walked the way she always walks, taller and straighter than anybody else. And I walked with my arm around her.

We walked all the way to the Tourist Office. Then we stopped for a minute and looked at the photo of San Pablo with all the houses of our town, pink and turquoise and pale green, and behind

58

them the blue lake and volcanoes and the high, rocky cliffs.

My grandmother looked at the writing under the picture. She touched it with her hand.

'What does it say?' she asked.

I read it to her. '"The Most Beautiful Place in the World."'

My grandmother looked surprised.

I started to wonder if San Pablo really was the most beautiful place in the world. I wasn't sure my grandmother had ever been anywhere else, but I still thought she'd know.

'Grandma,' I said, 'is it?'

'Is it what?' she said.

'Is San Pablo the most beautiful place in the world?'

My grandmother made a little face.

'The most beautiful place in the world,' she said, 'is any place.'

'Any place?' I repeated.

'Any place you can hold your head up. Any place you can be proud of who you are.'

'Yes,' I said.

But I thought, where you love somebody a whole lot, and you know that person loves you, that's the most beautiful place in the world.

THE END

GREEN MONSTER MAGIC

by Marjorie Newman

'This may be magic! Maybe he has a secret for you –
and for Joseph . . .'

Estelle's small brother, Joseph, is scared stiff at the
thought of acting in the school play. His Mum and
Dad will be there to see him – and Grandmother,
who is coming all the way from Africa on a visit!

How can Estelle help Joseph overcome his fear? She
doesn't know what to do, until a neighbour's story
about a crocodile, and a little green monster, gives
her a wonderful idea . . .

ISBN 0 552 52620 7

YOUNG
CORGI

PURR

by Jennifer Zabel

'URGENT!' said the notice. 'Kitten needs home by Friday. Going to Cat Sanctuary if not taken.'

Katy, Nick and their baby brother Ben are determined to have a kitten – even though Dad *hates* cats! And how can Mum not help when they see the sad little sign in the pet shop?

But once the small tabby kitten arrives home, the children realize that they have a new problem. For not only does the naughty little kitten appear to do its best to upset Dad, but it also seems to be rather lonely. Maybe they now need a second kitten to keep him company . . .

ISBN 0 552 52545 6

YOUNG CORGI